Please return/renew this item by the last date
shown. Books may be renewed by
telephoning, writing to or calling in at any
library or on the Internet.

Hurricane Season

by David Orme and Doreen Lang

Evans

FOR ANGELA

First published 2007
Evans Brothers Limited
2A Portman Mansions
Chiltern St
London W1U 6NR

British Library Cataloguing in Publication Data
Orme, David, 1948 Mar. 1-
   Hurricane season. - (Skylarks)
   1. Hurricanes - Juvenile fiction 2. Children's stories
   I. Title
   823.9'14[J]

   ISBN-13: 9780237533892 (hb)
   ISBN-13: 9780237534073 (pb)
   Printed in China by WKT Co. Ltd.

Series Editor: Louise John
Design: Robert Walster
Production: Jenny Mulvanny

Contents

Chapter One

"It's small, but we like it!"

Grandpa stood back to let the family in. Grace jumped in first, followed by Mum and Dad.

"I love it!" Grace said.

Grandma and Grandpa lived in New York. In the winter they shut up their apartment and drove down to their trailer in Florida to enjoy the sunshine. This year, they had come early because their granddaughter, Grace, and her Mum and Dad had come to Florida from England for a holiday.

"We're really sorry you can't stay with us in the trailer, Grace," said Grandma.

"There's just not much room!"

Mum and Dad and Grace were staying in a holiday hotel in West Palm Beach. It was near the sea. It was great but Grace really loved the trailer.

"I'd really, really like to stay here." Grandma looked at Mum.

"Why not? There would be room for Grace. Why don't you two have a couple of days by yourself and leave Grace with us? We'd love to have her."

Just then a thin man in a baseball cap came over.

"This is Rick," Grandpa said. "He's the park supervisor. He looks after everything for us and chases the alligators away!"

Rick laughed and shook hands with Grace, Mum and Dad. Then his face changed. He looked serious.

"Have you heard the news, Bob?"

"Nope," said Grandpa. "What's going on?"

"Hurricane coming. It's gonna be a biggie, too."

Chapter Two

Grandma and Grandpa weren't used to hurricanes. They usually came to Florida in winter, when the hurricane season was over.

"Is it coming this way?"

"We should be OK," said Rick. "They say it'll first hit land about a hundred miles up the coast, near Daytona Beach. It'll be stormy, so tie everything down, and don't make plans to go anywhere, but it shouldn't be too bad."

Grace looked worried.

"I can still stay, can't I, Grandpa? I don't mind storms!"

Grandpa laughed.

"We'd love to have you. If your Mum and Dad are happy, we are."

Mum didn't really like the idea of Grace sleeping in the trailer when there were hurricanes about, even if they were a hundred miles away. But she could see how much Grace wanted to stay.

"We're not far away," Dad said. "We can come and get you anytime."

They had a great day at the trailer park, though the weather wasn't very good. Yesterday had been sunny, but now there was a lot of wind and cloud.

The park was very small. There were twelve

trailers, a wooden hut where Rick kept his tools, and a small brick building that hummed and had cables coming out of it. Most of the trailers were empty.

"Most of the people here only come for the winter," said Grandma.

All around the park was the Everglades. This was nothing like the woods that Grace knew in England. The ground was squelchy, and the branches were covered with hanging green plants.

"That's called Spanish Moss," Grandma said. "It grows everywhere."

"Are there really alligators here?" asked Grace.

"There are quite a few near the river, where it is really swampy. Do you remember the little wooden bridge you came over to get in the park? You often see one there. The main road you came along is called 'Alligator Alley'."

After they had a look round Grandpa got the barbecue going. This was hard because the wind was getting stronger all the time.

"Now for some proper American hamburgers!" he said.

Chapter Three

Grace loved sleeping in the trailer. At first it had been hard to sleep, especially with the wind blowing outside. She had wondered how bad it would get. She usually quite liked storms, especially if she was safe inside.

She woke suddenly. Grandma was shaking her arm.

"Grace, wake up. Get dressed quickly, please!"

"What's going on?"

"Nothing to worry about. We've got to leave, that's all."

Grace got dressed. She could hear heavy rain beating on the roof of the trailer.

Grandpa came in, wearing heavy-duty waterproofs.

"What are you doing, Grandpa?"

"Loading the car. It's the hurricane, Grace. It changed direction. It's coming straight this way. It's going to hit this area some time this evening. We're going to have to stay with your mum and dad in the hotel. Are you ready?

Leaving in ten minutes!"

The car was just outside the trailer, but it was raining so hard that Grace was quickly soaked. She had never seen rain like it. The wind was so fierce even Grandpa's big SUV was shaking.

"Everybody in? Right, let's go," said Grandpa.

But the car wouldn't start.

Chapter Four

"I'll go and see if Rick's still around," said Grandpa.

But Rick had already gone. The trailer park was deserted.

Grandpa tried ringing a breakdown service, but no one answered. Everyone was busy because of the hurricane.

"You'd better ring Julie and Mike," said Grandma.

Grace, tucked up in the back of the car, felt ashamed. She hadn't given Mum and Dad a thought. They would be worried. But it was only a storm. Nothing awful could happen. But Grandma's face showed that it could.

"Mike? Yes, we're all here. You've seen the hurricane warning? Yes, headed straight this way. Look, the car won't start. What did you say? Coming here? Mike, be careful!"

"Grace is fine," he continued. "I'm sure I'll get hold of a garage soon. OK, but be careful. See you later."

"He's coming over to pick us up,"
Grandpa told them.

Three hours later Dad still hadn't
arrived, and the storm was getting worse
and worse.

Chapter Five

As soon as Grace's dad reached the
turnpike he knew he was in trouble.
People were trying to get away and the
road was clogged with cars. The wind
and rain made driving very difficult, and
people were driving slowly.

After a few miles everything stopped.
Mr Jordan sat and sat. At last he turned
the engine off.

He thought he'd better let everyone
know what had happened so he reached
into his pocket for his phone.

His pocket was empty. The phone was
lying on the table in the hotel. Mr
Jordan began to feel desperate. He was

trapped in traffic with the wind and rain getting worse and worse. He couldn't even let people know what was going on.

Chapter Six

At lunchtime Grandpa and Grandma
decided to ring the hotel. Mr Jordan had
been on the road for four hours.

"Julie? It's me. Look, I don't want
to worry you, but Mike hasn't got
here yet."

Even over the crackly mobile phone Grace could tell how worried Mum was.

"It's the roads. I've been watching the television. There's been... accidents. The traffic is backed up for miles. Mike left his phone behind. I can't get in touch with him."

"Julie, don't worry. I'm sure Mike'll be OK. I'll ring you as soon as he gets here. I want to save the battery so I'll go now. Don't worry. Everything will be fine, trust me."

Grace had loved the trailer at first, but now she was beginning to hate it. When Rick had left he had turned off the park's electricity. Grandma had hung up a gas lamp, but the light was gloomy. With every gust of wind the trailer shook. The rain drummed on the metal roof. Grace had seen pictures of hurricane damage. Houses with roofs torn off. Trailers blown over and wrecked.

Two more hours passed. By mid-afternoon the wind was roaring. How much longer could the trailer stay upright? Then they heard a car horn, and there was Dad, waving to them from the car.

Chapter Seven

"Let's get off straight away. The worst winds will be at eight o'clock tonight. If we go now, we'll be fine; the road is clear now," he shouted.

Grandpa rang Grace's mum, who sounded close to panic. Then they hurried out into the wind and rain. Grace had never known wind like it. She hung on to her dad.

"It was a nightmare. A truck had skidded and blocked the road. There was so much traffic they had a job to get a breakdown truck to clear it away."

"Don't worry, Mike. You did a great job. Now, let's get rolling."

The track down to the bridge had become a mud bath. It was hard to see where they were going. The windscreen wipers were going as fast as they could, but even that wasn't fast enough.

Suddenly Grandpa let out a yell. "Mike, stop, now!"

Mr Jordan stepped on the brake too

hard, and the car started to skid down
the track. It stopped right on the edge
of the river.

The wooden bridge had been
swept away.

Chapter Eight

At last, skidding and sliding, they made it back to the trailer. Grandpa stayed outside with Dad for a talk.

"We're in big trouble now, Mike. I'm going to call 911. We've got to get help."

But the message on the screen of the phone said *No Service*.

"What's wrong?"

"I expect the phone mast has come down in the wind."

"Would we be safer in the SUV than the trailer?"

"Might be. It won't blow over. It's stuff flying around that causes most problems. The windows could get smashed."

The two men went into the trailer. There was no point in hiding the bad news. They were in serious danger.

"The problem is that the dirt track is the only way out of here. And there are no buildings strong enough to shelter in. We'll have to get into the SUV and ride out the hurricane there."

Then Grace spoke up.

"What about that little brick place? The one with the wires coming out of it? That looked strong."

"Grace, you're brilliant!" said Grandpa. "The power room! We'd be safe there."

Just then a huge gust of wind shook the trailer, and they heard a grating noise from underneath. Some plates slid off the table and smashed.

"Quick, let's go. Rick's shed first, if it's still there. We'll need a crowbar to break down the door of the power room."

There was less rain now, but it was almost impossible to stand upright. Mr Jordan hung on tightly to Grace as they fought their way across the park.

Then they saw the alligators, four or five of them, lying on the ground between themselves and the wooden hut, their yellow eyes open and alert.

Chapter Nine

It was hard to be heard against the howling wind.

"The floods have brought them out," Grandpa yelled. "The river's too high even for 'gators."

"How dangerous are they?"

"Hard to say. You don't see them that often. Rick says sometimes you can walk right past and they will ignore you. Other times they will go for you."

"What do we do?"

"We'll work our way round the park, behind the vans, on the side away from the river. Let's hope there are no 'gators

38

hiding in the trees. Now, hold hands."

It was an awful journey. Grace was terrified that a trailer would be blown over as they struggled past, or that an alligator with flashing teeth would leap out at them.

It took half an hour to work their way round to Rick's hut. When they got

there they found the door had blown open. Grandpa went in and found the tool he needed.

"This hut isn't going to last much longer. Let's break open the power room door and get out of this wind!"

Chapter Ten

It had been a horrible night in the power room. A large machine took up most of the space. Nobody slept. And when they went out in the morning they couldn't believe they were in the same place.

Not one trailer was still standing. It looked as if a huge, angry dinosaur had

smashed its way through the park.

The SUV didn't look too damaged, but when they reached it they saw every window had been smashed. They would have been killed if they had stayed in it.

As they stood there, a US coastguard helicopter roared overhead.

Someone in an orange suit came down towards them on a cable.

Grace looked at where their trailer had been and burst into tears. Grandma held her tightly.

"We can get another trailer any time. We can't get another granddaughter. Especially one who had such a good idea it saved all our lives!"

If you enjoyed this story, why not read another *Skylarks* book?

London's Burning

by Pauline Francis
and Alessandro Baldanzi

It was dark in the attic bedroom and John really wanted a candle. He sneaked downstairs and stole the candle from his parents' bedroom. John slept soundly with his candle flickering on the windowsill beside him. But in the morning when he woke, the air was thick with smoke and the smell of burning. London was on fire! And John's candle had disappeared…

Sleeping Beauty

By Louise John and Natascia Ugliano

After a curse is placed upon her as a baby, a princess pricks her finger on a spinning wheel and falls into a deep sleep on her sixteenth birthday. The rest of the palace falls into a deep sleep with her. One hundred years later, a handsome prince rides past the forgotten palace. Will the prince be able to undo the curse and finally awaken the princess?

Skylarks titles include:

Awkward Annie
by Julia Williams and Tim Archbold
HB 9780237533847
PB 9780237534028

Sleeping Beauty
by Louise John and Natascia Ugliano
HB 9780237533861
PB 9780237534042

Detective Derek
by Karen Wallace and Beccy Blake
HB 9780237533885
PB 9780237534066

Hurricane Season
by David Orme and Doreen Lang
HB 9780237533892
PB 9780237534073

Spiggy Red
by Penny Dolan and Cinzia Battistel
HB 9780237533854
PB 9780237534035

London's Burning
by Pauline Francis and Alessandro Baldanzi
HB 9780237533878
PB 9780237534059